# TONI MORRISON
## & SLADE MORRISON

# Please, Louise

Illustrated by
## SHADRA STRICKLAND

A Paula Wiseman Book
SIMON & SCHUSTER
BOOKS FOR YOUNG READERS
New York London Toronto Sydney New Delhi

SIMON & SCHUSTER BOOKS FOR YOUNG READERS
An imprint of Simon & Schuster Children's Publishing Division
1230 Avenue of the Americas, New York, New York 10020
Text copyright © 2014 by Toni Morrison and the Estate of Slade Morrison
Illustrations copyright © 2014 by Shadra Strickland

For information about special discounts for bulk purchases,
please contact Simon & Schuster Special Sales at 1-866-506-1949 or business@simonandschuster.com.
The Simon & Schuster Speakers Bureau can bring authors to your live event.
For more information or to book an event, contact the Simon & Schuster Speakers Bureau
at 1-866-248-3049 or visit our website at www.simonspeakers.com.
Also available in a Simon & Schuster Books for Young Readers hardcover edition
Book design by Laurent Linn
The text for this book is set in Minister Std.
The illustrations for this book are rendered in watercolor, gouache, pencil, and crayon.
Manufactured in China
1215 SCP
First Simon & Schuster Books for Young Readers paperback edition March 2016
2 4 6 8 10 9 7 5 3 1
The Library of Congress has cataloged the hardcover edition as follows:
Morrison, Toni.
Please, Louise / Toni Morrison ; Slade Morrison ; illustrated by Shadra Strickland. — 1st ed.
p. cm.
"A Paula Wiseman Book."
Summary: On a gray, rainy day, everything seems particularly frightening and bad to Louise until she enters a
library and finds books that help her to know and imagine the beauty and wonder that have been there all along.
ISBN 978-1-4169-8338-5 (hardcover : alk. paper) — ISBN 978-1-4169-8339-2 (pbk)
ISBN 978-1-4424-3310-6 (eBook)
[1. Books and reading—Fiction. 2. Fear—Fiction. 3. Libraries—Fiction.] I. Morrison, Slade.
II. Strickland, Shadra, ill. III. Title.
PZ7.M845147Ple 2013
[E]—dc23
2012026303

For librarians everywhere
—*T. M.*

For August, Chainey, Hannah, and Jersey Rose, with love
—*S. S.*

Please, Louise, please, please.
Things are not always what they seem.
If you are sometimes lonely or sometimes sad,
know that the world is big but not so bad.

The sky is gray now but not for long.
After the rain, birds break into song.
Please, Louise, please, please.
There's nothing hiding in those trees.

Don't scurry too fast and miss the music of the street.
You may be surprised by who or what you meet.

You frown at the yard where that old car is parked
and shrink from the sound of a little dog's bark.

Is that house really haunted? Or does it just need care?
Why not imagine the joy that used to be there?

Is that a junkyard? Or a dangerous trap,
where ghosts live and monsters nap?
Scary thoughts are your creation
when you have no information.

Sheets of rain, black clouds, thunder.

Hurry! Find a roof to get under!

Is that a bird of prey from which you'd better run?

Or an eagle of gold when touched by the sun?

A library is shelter from any storm.
In that place you are never alone.

These books are loyal friends, helping you explore,
dream, discover, think, learn, and know much, much more.

Imagination is an open door.
Step in here and let it soar.

"Venice is a city that sits in the sea. . . ."

"When pirate ships sailed the ocean lanes . . ."

"Dolphins are the most social . . ."

"The princess sat weeping in her chamber . . ."

"Juju the lion cub was lost.

He could not find his mother . . ."

See, little girl, this is your world.
So smile awhile as the stories unfurl
where beauty and wonder cannot hide.
Because reading books is a pleasing guide.

Fear and sadness—where did they go?
Louise doesn't care. Louise doesn't know.

She can understand what she feels,
since books can teach and please Louise.

# On the day you were born

Margaret Wild & Ron Brooks

ALLEN & UNWIN

SYDNEY · MELBOURNE · AUCKLAND · LONDON

*My daddy said,*
On the day you were born, I wrapped you up warm
and took you for a walk to see the world.

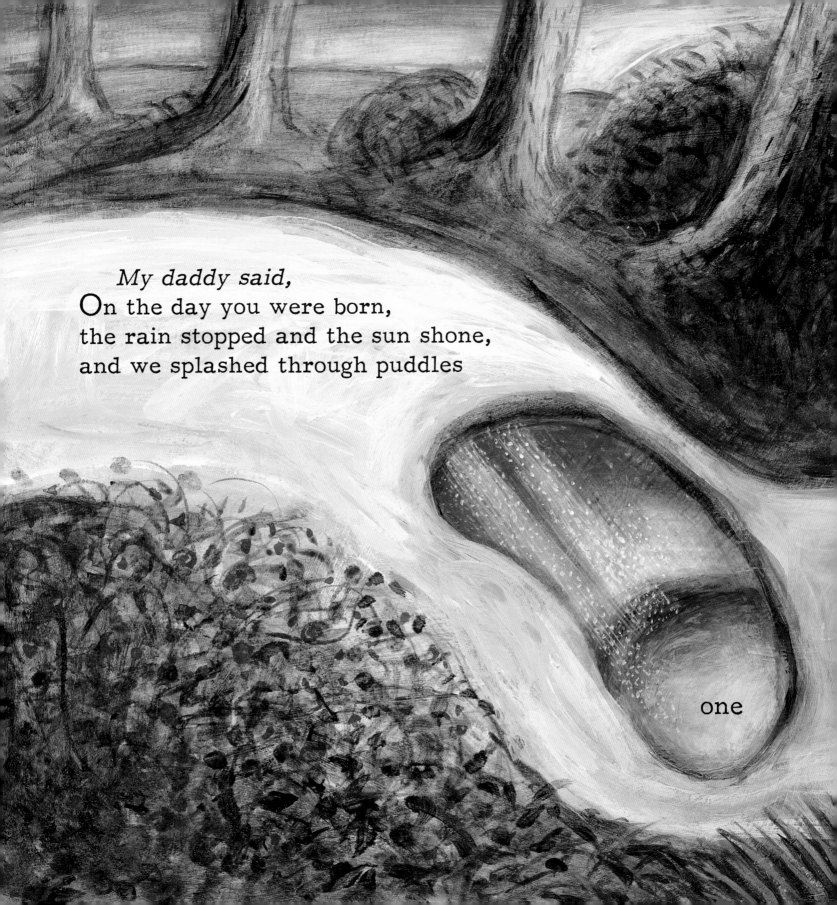

*My daddy said,*
On the day you were born,
the rain stopped and the sun shone,
and we splashed through puddles

one

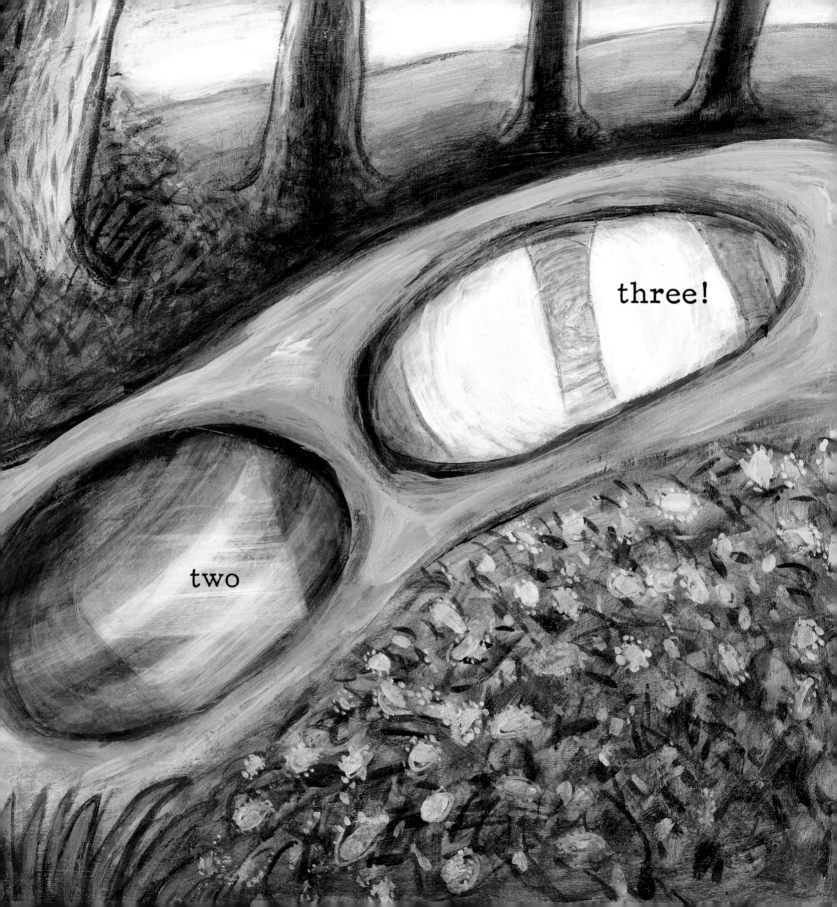

*My daddy said,*
On the day you were born,
some of the night creatures,
Owl and Mouse and Bat,
woke up and poked out their heads
to say a sleepy hello.

*My daddy said,*
On the day you were born,
we followed the bees,
and all around us was humming
and the glorious smell of honey.

*My daddy said,*
On the day you were born,
there was a duckling all alone in the river,
and we watched and waited
until it swam quacking back to its family.

*My daddy said,*
On the day you were born, we sat by a creaky,
crackly old tree - a granddaddy tree! -
and I told you that it was here
I first met your mother.

*My daddy said,*
On the day you
were born,

our friends wanted to kiss and cuddle,

squish and squeeze you so lovingly that I had to rescue you!

*My daddy said,*
On the day you were born,
falcons and hawks did acrobatics in the sky,
and a feather fell to earth,
right into your hand.

*My daddy said,*
On the day you were born,
the bushes were bright with berries -

and I longed to pop one in your mouth
and see you wriggle with surprise and delight.

*My daddy said,*
On the day you were born,
you lay quietly among the wildflowers,

entranced by ladybirds and butterflies
while the crickets sang.

*My daddy said,*
On the day you were born,
the moon was full and white and
sumptuous as it lit our way safely home.

*My daddy said,*
On the day you were born,
I put you back in your mother's arms,
and that night we were the world,
the three of us together.